Sad Superhero

A Book About Facing Emotions

By Emily Marck

To Grandpa, whose smile always made me smile. He is the maker of the dollhouse seen in this book.

The wind rustled the grass on Annie Tear's lawn as the clouds above played hide and seek with the sun. It was a perfect day for anyone in the town of Powerfeel, except for Annie Tear. She looked at the sky with disinterest and felt the windblown grass looked a little dull in color.

Annie Tear plopped herself onto her porch swing with a sigh. Her sister Daisy would be coming home for the first time in a long while. She knew she should be excited, but she was mostly worried. Daisy was very special—so special that everyone in Powerfeel knew her name.

Annie Tear's sister Daisy was sweet, smart, smiley, and so, so strong. She could do anything she wanted, but there was a reason for this. Daisy was a superhero. She had the power to take away and give emotions to people with a click of her fingers.

Daisy usually flew high above the town looking for people whose feelings were hurt. She flew down from the sky when the townsfolk were grumpy after a long day at work or when they were angry at their friends or crying alone. Then she would snap her fingers, and they were filled with joy again.

Annie Tear was different though. She was what everyone called an UN-superhero. She was the exact opposite of Daisy. No matter how many times Daisy clicked her fingers for Annie Tear, she remained sad. So the people of Powerfeel stopped calling her just Annie. They renamed her. She was now known as Annie Tear.

"Why do I get the worst of everything when she gets the best?" Annie Tear whispered. As she said this, a great wind made the porch swing creak loudly and thrust her back and forth. Annie didn't even bother to look up as she was jerked to a stop suddenly. She knew what the wind was already.

"Hi, Daisy," Annie Tear said with a sigh.

Daisy sat down next to her sister. "Sorry about the wind. Are you okay?"

"I'm fine," Annie Tear said as she looked up at Daisy. But when she saw her face, Annie Tear realized something was definitely not right. Daisy looked tired and wasn't wearing her usual smile. Worst of all, she said,

"I need your help, Annie Tear."

"My help?" Annie Tear said. "But I'm an UN-Superhero, and you're hero of the town. Why would you need me?"

Daisy lowered her voice and whispered softly, "Because I just met the first supervillain to ever enter Powerfeel."

Annie Tear gasped and a shiver went up her spine. "What do we do?"

"First, we'll have go to my good feelings storage room where I can tell you my plan in secret. Take my hand," Daisy said in a strong voice. She offered a hand to Annie Tear. Daisy took flight as Annie Tear clung onto Daisy's hand, and they rose into the air.

"So this is what it is like to be a superhero, to fly into the bright white clouds like a bird," thought Annie Tear. She almost felt herself be something other then glum—maybe content. But then a new thought entered her head. "I'll never fly like this on my own. I'm an UN-superhero. This is never going to happen again."

All of a sudden, the white clouds turned pink and rainbow bubbles hovered around Annie Tear and Daisy. The change in the clouds had happened so quickly, Annie Tear was sure that Daisy had caused it.

"Did you click your fingers and make the clouds happy?" Annie Tear asked, not sure what else could have happened. But Daisy laughed. "No, silly. I have the power to find invisible good feelings. They are patches coming from the clouds in the sky."

Daisy let go of Annie Tear's hand, and she felt herself standing in thin air with pink clouds and rainbow bubbles floating around her. Annie Tear looked at Daisy, who seemed to be deep in thought.

"If we are going to stop the supervillain, we will need all the happy bubbles in my storage," Daisy said while clicking her fingers.

As the rainbow bubbles flew into Daisy's palms and sank into her hands, an awful thought entered Annie Tear's head.

"What do I do to stop him? You have your powers and your happy bubbles. I don't have anything." Annie Tear felt defeat filling her heart.

At this, Daisy looked sad. Then she whispered, "It is impossible for you to help me."

"What do you mean? You asked for my help," Annie Tear whispered as a tear fell down her cheek.

"I was hoping the energy that fills these clouds would finally make you happy. I figured if you became happy, you might turn into a superhero. Then you would have been able to help me," Daisy whispered. "I'm sorry. I was wrong. Now I realize I can't help you. You will have to be the one to make yourself happy, not me."

As Daisy flew Annie Tear back home, she tried to make her sister feel better.

"You know, I think everything will be alright. I'll defeat the supervillain, and you'll make yourself happy on your own. We all have different battles."

"Except mine never end in applause," Annie Tear said with a scowl.

Annie Tear's chest felt hollow as she quickly found her adventure with Daisy was over.

"Are you going to be okay?" Daisy asked lightly with a worried sigh in her voice. "Don't worry. I'll care take of the supervillain and stop him before he can make anyone else sad."

"Is that his evil power? To make people sad?" Annie Tear asked. Suddenly, she felt angry and excited at the same moment. "Of course I can help! You didn't even think about what I can do! I am immune to this supervillain's power. I'm already sad. There is nothing bad he can do to me!"

Daisy looked at Annie Tear in shock. Then finally she smiled.

"I guess we will be a superhero team on this one!" Daisy said as she took Annie Tear's hand in hers. They were off again. As Daisy and Annie Tear landed in the center of town, an evil cackle that sounded as horrible as a nightmare but also as sad as a bad day, met their ears.

"So you've come again, superhero," the supervillain said in a sniffly voice. "It's time for you to understand what it's like to be sad!" He lifted his hands and got ready to snap them in an evil way.

But Daisy was ready. She opened her palms, and the happy bubbles flew into his hands to stop his sad power.

But it didn't stop the supervillain one bit. All of a sudden, there was a click of fingers, and Daisy's triumphant smile turned into a frown. Then she started to cry. Annie Tear gasped in horror. But then, a thought struck her and she turned to the supervillain. Instead of looking triumphant, the supervillain just stood there in silence, looking miserable.

Suddenly, Annie Tear understood it all. She burst out, "You're sad, aren't you? You must be an UN-superhero like me! You want to make people sad so they can understand how you feel!"

At this, the supervillain stood even stiller than before. Then, a tear trickled down his cheek. A tear of relief.

"You understand? No one has before. You ARE like me!" he said, a sigh of contentedness in his voice. The ends of his mouth started to twitch, and a half smile came onto his face.

"I guess I'm not alone!" the supervillain said. His smile grew bigger.

For the first time in her life, Annie Tear started to smile too. "I guess I'm not alone either," Annie Tear said with much relief in her voice.

Daisy suddenly turned to look at Annie Tear and began to smile again. "You're smiling!" said a shocked Daisy to Annie Tear. "And so is the supervillain!"

Annie Tear turned to him and said, "What's your name? I can't just call you 'supervillain.'"

"I'm Dennis," he said as he turned to face Annie Tear.

"You do have a superpower, Annie Tear. You have the power to feel empathy and understand how people feel. That's the way you'll help people," Dennis said.

"We all can do that if we try," said Superhero Annie. "And we can all be superheroes!"

So the three superheroes laughed and smiled, and they became a superhero trio!

Sad Superhero tells the story of two sisters with two different battles. Daisy, the superhero, has to stop a supervillain to save the town of Powerfeel, while Annie Tear must battle her emotions. Both battles are very important, and soon they will both learn that they can work together to reach the end of their battles side by side.

Made in the USA
Middletown, DE
11 February 2023

24606511R00020